DISCARD

At 9:59 on Thursday morning,
Jodie drew a duck. She gave the
duck a top hat, cane, and boots
of the softest leather.
On the boots, she put silver buttons:
one . . . two . . .

Her pen hovered in the air
before the final button.

To Rosie, who drew me the duck

First U.S. edition 2013

Library of Congress Catalog Card Number 2012947825
ISBN 978-0-7636-6437-4

13 14 15 16 17 18 CCP 10 9 8 7 6 5 4 3 2

Printed in Shenzhen, Guangdong, China

This book was typeset in Bembo.
The illustrations were done in ink and watercolor.

Candlewick Press
99 Dover Street
Somerville, Massachusetts 02144

visit us at www.candlewick.com

The Silver Button

BOB GRAHAM

CANDLEWICK PRESS

Jodie's brother, Jonathan, pushed slowly to his feet.

He swayed, he frowned,

he tilted forward . . .

and took his first step.

He took that step like he was
going somewhere.

At that moment, Jodie and Jonathan's mom began to play "Merrily Kiss the Quaker's Wife" on her pennywhistle.

Mom loved the picture of the wild hare on her calendar so much, she hadn't changed it in three years.

Outside,
a pigeon nested
under the roof.
As Jonathan took
his first step,
a feather floated
gently past the
window like an
autumn leaf.

Next door,
Alice mailed sticks
and stones through
the front gate . . .

and an early-morning
jogger puffed on by.

Out in the street, Joseph Pascano avoided the cracks
in the sidewalk so the sharks wouldn't get him.

An ambulance shrieked past Jodie's house.

On High Street,
Bernard had his shoelace
tied for the second time
that morning . . .

and a man bought some fresh bread
from the baker.

One block away, a soldier
said good-bye to his mom.

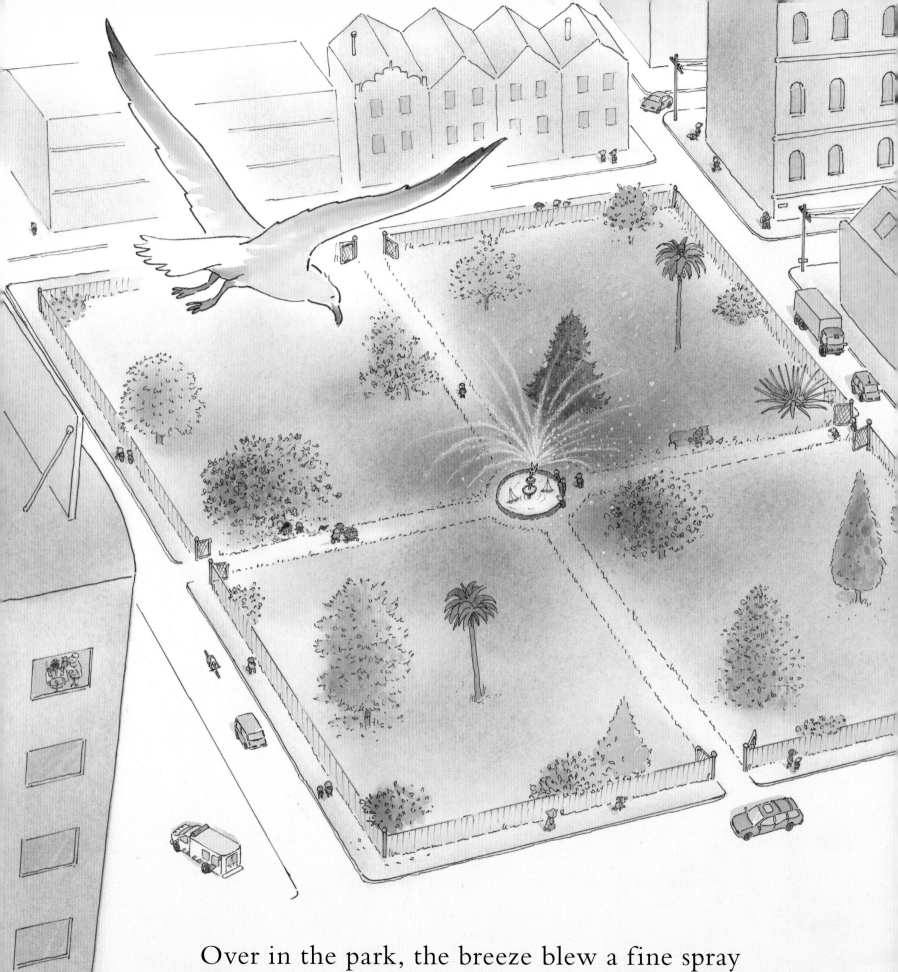

Over in the park, the breeze blew a fine spray
over children sailing boats in the fountain.

Under the oak,
Sophie and her granddad
made a house of leaves.
Sophie sat in the living room
while Granddad swept
the bedroom.

On the edge of the path,
a blackbird found a worm . . .

and an old lady
shuffled by, pushing
everything she
owned in her cart.

High over the city, a flight of ducks headed south like an arrow.

In Mercy Hospital, a baby was born.

Over on City Beach,
Belle and Vashti
popped seaweed.

On the shoreline,
Paddy dried off while
Jock scratched his back
in the sand.

Sunlight hit the windows
of the city, and phones rang
in a thousand offices
and pockets.

Far out over the bay,
a tanker headed all the way to China.

Then down came Jonathan

on his little pink knees.

"Mommy!" yelled Jodie.
"Jonathan's just taken his first step."

Jodie put the last silver button
on her duck's boots.

Sunlight from all over the city
streamed through the window,
and the kitchen clock
struck ten.